Knowsley Library Service

Please return this book on or
before the date shown below

Due
8.10.20

1 6 SEP 2022

7 MAR 2023

2 1 NOV 2023

0 2 JAN 2024

1 4 AUG 2023

Read more DRAGON books!

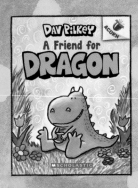

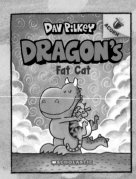

DRAGON's
Fat Cat

DaV PiLKeY

ACORN™
SCHOLASTIC

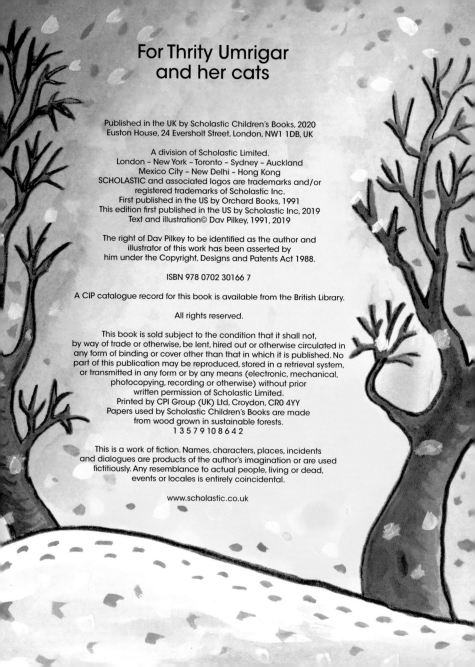

For Thrity Umrigar
and her cats

Published in the UK by Scholastic Children's Books, 2020
Euston House, 24 Eversholt Street, London, NW1 1DB, UK

A division of Scholastic Limited.
London – New York – Toronto – Sydney – Auckland
Mexico City – New Delhi – Hong Kong
SCHOLASTIC and associated logos are trademarks and/or
registered trademarks of Scholastic Inc.
First published in the US by Orchard Books, 1991
This edition first published in the US by Scholastic Inc, 2019
Text and illustration© Dav Pilkey, 1991, 2019

The right of Dav Pilkey to be identified as the author and
illustrator of this work has been asserted by
him under the Copyright, Designs and Patents Act 1988.

ISBN 978 0702 30166 7

A CIP catalogue record for this book is available from the British Library.

Printed by CPI Group (UK) Ltd, Croydon, CR0 4YY
Papers used by Scholastic Children's Books are made
from wood grown in sustainable forests.
1 3 5 7 9 10 8 6 4 2

This is a work of fiction. Names, characters, places, incidents
and dialogues are products of the author's imagination or are used
fictitiously. Any resemblance to actual people, living or dead,
events or locales is entirely coincidental.

www.scholastic.co.uk

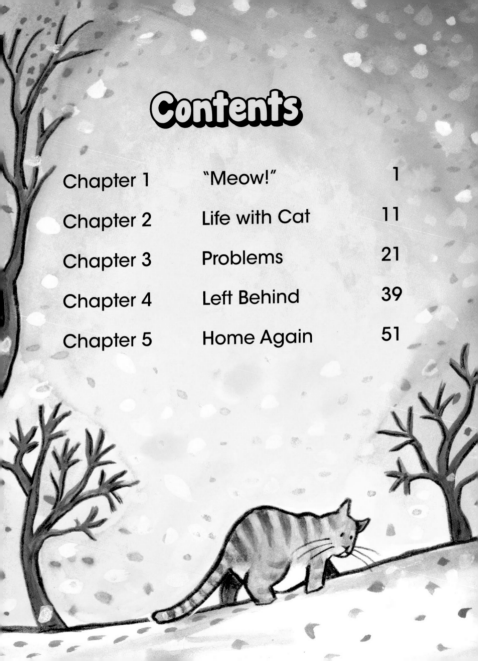

Contents

1
"Meow!"

One snowy day in January,
Dragon heard a funny noise.

"Meow!"

"That sounds like a cat," said Dragon.

3

He opened his door and looked outside.
Out in the garden, sitting in the snow,
was a fat grey cat.

"Hello, little cat," said Dragon.
"Come inside and get warm."

But the fat cat did not come inside.
The fat cat just sat in the snow and said,
"Meow."

5

Later, Dragon heard another funny noise.

"Meow!"

"There's that cat again," said Dragon.

"Won't you please come inside
and get warm?" Dragon asked.

But the fat cat did not come inside.
The fat cat just sat in the snow and said,
"Meow!"

The day passed, and Dragon did not hear
any more funny noises.

When Dragon looked outside,
he did not see the fat cat.
All he could see was a blanket of snow
with a fat lump in the middle.

"Oh, no!" said Dragon.
"Something is not right."

Dragon went outside
and scooped away at the snow.
He scooped and scooped and scooped
until he found the fat cat.

"You are coming with me," said Dragon.
And he took the cold cat inside.

2
Life with Cat

After a few hours by the fire,
the fat cat was warm, dry and very cosy.
The fat cat sat in Dragon's lap
and purred and purred.

"It is too cold for you
to go back outside," said Dragon.
"So you will have to stay here with me."

The fat cat did not seem to mind.

14

"And if you are going to stay with me,"
Dragon said,
"I will have to give you a name."

Dragon tried to think of a name
for the fat cat.

"I will call you Cat," said Dragon.

Cat was a very good name for a cat.

"If you are going to live at my house,"
said Dragon,
"you will need a bed to sleep in."

So Dragon took a big brown basket
and filled it with soft blankets.
Then he wrote Cat's name on the side.

17

Dragon put Cat's bed down on the floor next to his own bed.

"How do you like your new bed?" Dragon asked.

But Cat was already fast asleep.

And soon, so was Dragon.

3
Problems

Dragon liked living with Cat,
and Cat liked living with Dragon.

But Dragon did not know
how to take care of Cat.

He did not know how to train Cat.

That was a problem.

Dragon did not know what to feed Cat.

That was a big problem.

24

And Dragon did not know what to do
about all the yellow puddles Cat made.

That was a smelly problem.

Dragon tried to teach Cat to use the toilet.

But Cat did not understand.

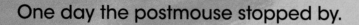

One day the postmouse stopped by.

"P.U.!" said the postmouse.
"Your house stinks!"

"I know," said Dragon.
"My cat has a smelly problem."

"What you need is a litter box,"
said the postmouse.
"A litter box will make
the smelly problem go away."

"A litter box?" said Dragon.
"That's a good idea."

So Dragon and Cat walked to the highway and picked up all the litter they could find.

Dragon put the litter into a box . . .

. . . and placed the box in his house.

Now Dragon's house **really** smelled bad.

Dragon did not know what to do.

"We need to go to the pet store,"
he told Cat.

So Dragon and Cat got into the car
and drove to the pet store.

"I need to buy some cat stuff,"
said Dragon.

"What's your cat's name?"
asked the sales pig.

"Cat," said Dragon.

"That's a good name for a cat,"
said the pig.

"I thought of it myself," said Dragon.

The kind old pig showed Dragon
how to take care of a cat.
She showed Dragon what to feed his cat.
And she even showed Dragon
how to get rid of the smelly problem.

Dragon bought a lot of things for Cat.
He left the pet store with
everything he needed . . .

... except for one thing.

4
Left Behind

When Dragon came home,
he got his house ready for Cat.
He put out dishes of food and water.
He filled a box up with kitty litter.
And he scattered cat toys
all over the floor.

All the while, Dragon had a funny feeling.

"I feel like I've forgotten something,"
he said.

Suddenly, Dragon remembered
what he had forgotten.

"Cat!" he shouted.
"I left you behind!"

Dragon found his torch
and went outside to look for Cat.

"Cat! Cat!" he called.

But Cat was nowhere to be found.

Dragon looked and looked
all through the night,
but he could not find Cat.

Dragon sat down on an old crate
and began to cry.

He had lost his cat.

Suddenly, Dragon heard a funny noise.

"Meow!"

Dragon looked around and around,
but he could not see Cat anywhere.

Finally, Dragon looked down
into the old crate...
and there was Cat.

But Cat was not alone.
Deep inside the crate,
snuggling close to Cat,
were five little kittens.

"You had babies!" said Dragon.
"Oh, you are a good cat!"

49

Dragon picked up the old crate
and brought it back to his warm house.

5
Home Again

Later that night, Dragon made up
good names for all of the kittens.

He then made five small beds
and wrote each kitten's name on the side.

Dragon put the kittens' beds on the floor
next to his own bed.

"How do you like your new beds?"
he asked.

But the kittens were already fast asleep.

And soon, so was Dragon.

About the Author

 is the creator of the bestselling Dog Man and Captain Underpants series. He has written and illustrated many other books for young readers, including the Dumb Bunnies series, *The Hallo-Wiener*, *Dog Breath*, and *The Paperboy*, which is a Caldecott Honour book. Dav lives in the Pacific Northwest with his wife.

YOU CAN DRAW DRAGON!

1 Draw an arch and a backward letter "C." They should connect.

2 Add Dragon's eyes and nose. Put two horns on top of his head.

3 Draw Cat's head and back.

4 Add Cat's ears and face.

5 Draw Dragon's back, tail, and arm. Give him a smile. He is holding Cat!

6 Draw spikes on Dragon's back and tail. Add his leg and foot. Draw Cat's legs.

7 Give Cat whiskers and a tail. Add Dragon's other leg and foot.

8 Colour in your drawing!

WHAT'S YOUR STORY?

Dragon learns that caring for a pet takes a lot of work.
Imagine **you** have a new pet.
How would you take care of your pet?
How could Dragon and Cat help you?
Write and draw your story!

BONUS!

Try making your story just like Dav – with watercolours! Did you know that Dav taught himself how to watercolour when he was making the Dragon books?
He went to the supermarket, bought a children's watercolour set, and used it to paint the entire book series.